Our SPECIAL World

KEEPING SAFE

Liz Lennon

W
FRANKLIN WATTS
LONDON • SYDNEY

Contents

Franklin Watts

First published in Great Britain in 2016 by
The Watts Publishing Group

Copyright © The Watts Publishing Group, 2016

All rights reserved.

Series Editor: Sarah Peutrill   Consultant: Karina Philip
Cover Designer: Cathryn Gilbert   Designer: Will Dawes

ISBN: 978 1 4451 4827 4
Dewey number: 613.6
Printed in China

Franklin Watts
An imprint of
Hachette Children's Group
Part of The Watts Publishing Group
Carmelite House
50 Victoria Embankment
London EC4Y 0DZ

An Hachette UK Company
www.hachette.co.uk
www.franklinwatts.co.uk

FSC
www.fsc.org
MIX
Paper from
responsible sources
FSC® C104740

Picture credits: Dreamstime:- iportret: 13b, 24bc;
Julia Kuznetsova: 16br; Ia64: 11; Madartists: 22;
MJTH: 9r; Photodynamx: 19t; Serrnovik: 16l; Syda
Productions: front cover cl, 12. Fotolia:- Dragon
Images: 1, 8b; Monkey Business Images: front cover
r, 5bl, 24cr; Philidor: front cover l, 19b, 24cl; Andres
Rodrigues: 5tl, 24c. Getty Images: -Photofusion:17t.
Photofusion:-John Birdsall: 15b. Shutterstock:-
Dimitrov Boyan: 7tl, 24tr; Oleg Doroshin: 10tr; T
Dway: 17b; Fine Art: 13tc; Stephen Finn: 18cl, 18bl,
18br; flashgun: 7bl, 24tc; grafvision: 10bc; Ian 2010:
10cr; Oleksandr Korchahin: 15tc; Dan Kosmayer: 10tl;
Andreii M: 15tl; Robyn Mackenzie: 18cr; Malinka1:
8c; MJTH: 6; ostill: 5r, 24br; Pavel L Photo and Video:
14, 23; Pranch: 13tl; Viacheslav Rashevskyi: 10br; Egor
Shilov: 9cl; Spotmatik Ltd: 16tr; Serghei Starus: 7tr,
24bl; unpict: 10cl; Vector.com: 15tr; Tom Wang: 21;
wavebreakmedia: 4, 7br, 20, 24tl; Jaren Jai Wicklund:
front cover cr, 3; xstockersx: 10bl.
Every attempt has been made to clear copyright.
Should there be any inadvertent omission please apply
to the publisher for rectification.

Keeping safe

Everyone needs to be safe. This means you are not in danger of getting hurt.

We all have people that make us feel safe. Charlie feels safe with his dad. Who do you feel safe with?

People who keep you safe

There are lots of people who help you understand what is safe and what isn't.

Your parents or carers and your teachers help you to learn about keeping safe.

Other people in your local area will also help. Who are these people?

Too hot!

Your skin is very important.
It covers and protects everything
inside your body.

Hot things can hurt your skin.
Even the sun can burn you.

Hot water, ovens, irons and barbecues can burn you.

Why should you never play with candles or matches?

Sharp things

When you cut or graze your skin, it bleeds. This helps your skin to heal. But some cuts can be serious.

Scissors are only for cutting paper – nothing else! Don't walk or run with scissors.

Sanjet is using scissors safely. What is she doing?

It's fun to help in the kitchen. But knives can be sharp.

Always use sharp knives with a grown-up. Never cut things in your hand. Use a chopping board.

What other things can you think of that are sharp?

In your mouth

Your body needs food but some things can make us poorly if we eat them.

Which of these things are not safe to put in your mouth?

cleaning things

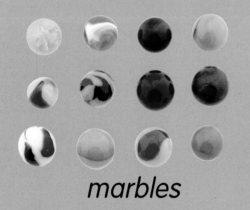
marbles

fruit

berries from a bush

biscuits

coins

scissors

Sometimes you have to take medicine. Only take medicine that is given to you by a grown-up.

The wrong medicine can make you very poorly.

Outside play

Under your skin are your bones. They are very strong – but they can still be broken. You can break your bones by falling from a height, like a climbing frame.

Choose climbing frames you feel safe on. Ask a grown-up if you're not sure.

If you think you or someone else has broken a bone:

Tell a grown-up.

Stay calm.

Don't try to move them.

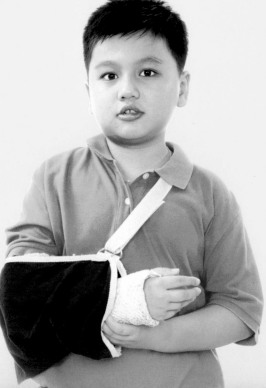

Charlie has a broken arm. It will take about five weeks to heal.

Crossing the road

Crossing the road can be very dangerous. Choose a safe place to cross.

Scarlet and Harry are using a zebra crossing.

What other safe places could you use?

Before you cross, remember to:

STOP!

LOOK!

LISTEN!

… just like
Anna and Carl.

On your bike

Riding your bike is great fun. These rules will help you keep safe on your bike.

Wear your cycle helmet.

Find a quiet place.

Drink water.

Be bright, be seen.

Be careful near animals.

Why should you be careful near animals?

By water

You must never go near water without a grown-up.

The dangers of water include:

It can be deep.

It may be moving fast.

Ice can break.

What do
you think
this means?

Ella is having fun on the water. She has
learned to swim. Learning to swim is the
best way to stay safe near water.
How else is she keeping safe?

Friends and bullies

Being safe is not just about things that hurt our bodies. We need to feel safe with people too.

Friends should always be kind to each other.

Ryan and Harry are friends. They enjoy being together.

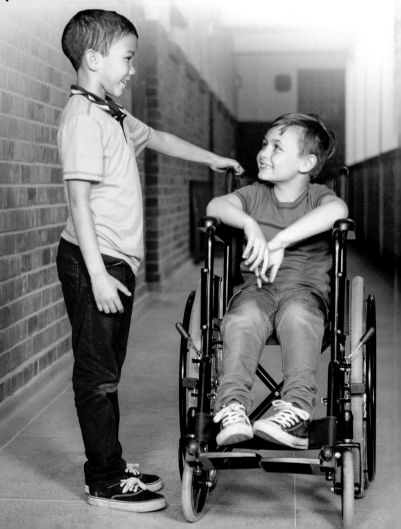

Bullies are people who are unkind. Tell a grown-up if you are ever bullied. And don't be a bully!

Alice has been mean to Amy. She hurt her feelings. What should Alice do?

Strangers

Keeping safe also means being aware which adults you should trust.

Before you go with anyone, even people you know, check first with your grown-up.

If someone tries to touch or talk to you and you feel unsafe, it is okay to say no. It's even okay to shout or kick them.

People, should never touch any part of your body that is covered by your swimsuit.

Who could you tell if this happens to you?

Word bank

 barbecue

 bath

 iron

 Life jacket

 Lollipop man

 Nurse

 Oven

 Plaster cast

 Police officer

Index